Reginald

Jeff Newman

A Doubleday Book for Young Readers

A Doubleday Book for Young Readers

Published by
Random House Children's Books
a division of
Random House, Inc.
New York

Doubleday and the anchor with dolphin colophon are registered trademarks of
Random House, Inc.

Visit us on the Web! www.randomhouse.com/kids
Educators and librarians, for a variety of teaching tools, visit us at
www.randomhouse.com/teachers

Cataloging-in-Publication data is available from the Library of Congress.
ISBN: 0-385-74634-2 (trade)
0-385-90862-8 (lib. bdg.)

The text of this book is set in 18-point Packard Bold.
Book design by Trish Parcell Watts
MANUFACTURED IN CHINA
October 2003
10 9 8 7 6 5 4 3 2 1

For Rachel

In the darkest depths of the Amazon, where snakes slither and bugs crawl, and hungry crocodiles snap their greedy jaws, there once lived . . .

. . . a cow.

Actually, *he* was a bull, but no one in
the jungle seemed to know the difference,
and he was too polite to point it out.
His name was Reginald. It said so on
his mailbox.

Now, Reginald lived in the very heart of the most inhospitable land known to cowkind.

His neighbor to the north was a jaguar, who feasted on animals that looked a lot like Reginald.

To the west lived a family of vampire bats, who stayed up every night playing poker and making horrible sucking sounds until the wee hours of the morning.

A poisonous old frog and his gecko underlings lived in a swamp to the east. They took pleasure in teasing Reginald, calling him names that are completely unprintable.

Lastly, to the south lived the worst of them all—an oversized, lunatic ape, who did nothing but stare into Reginald's home all day long and say, "I'm gonna eatcha."

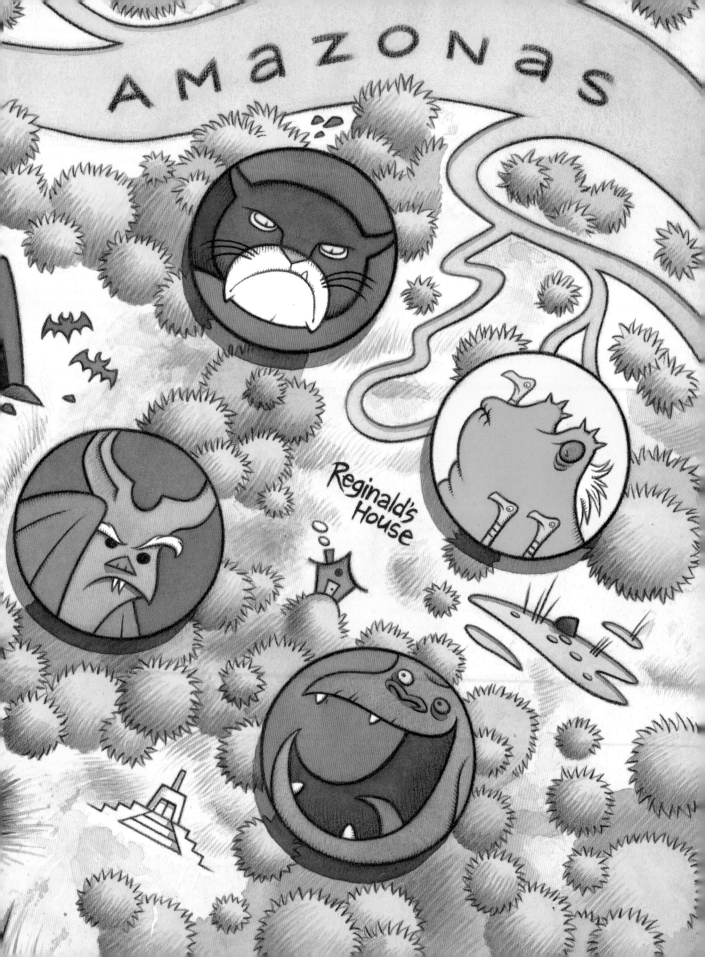

Most civilized animals would have wobbled like jelly under such circumstances, but none of it seemed to bother Reginald very much. Every morning, he made his way down to the river and enjoyed a fine breakfast of leaves and water.

When he returned home, he sat in his favorite chair and read, or wrote, or simply looked out the window and enjoyed the scenery.

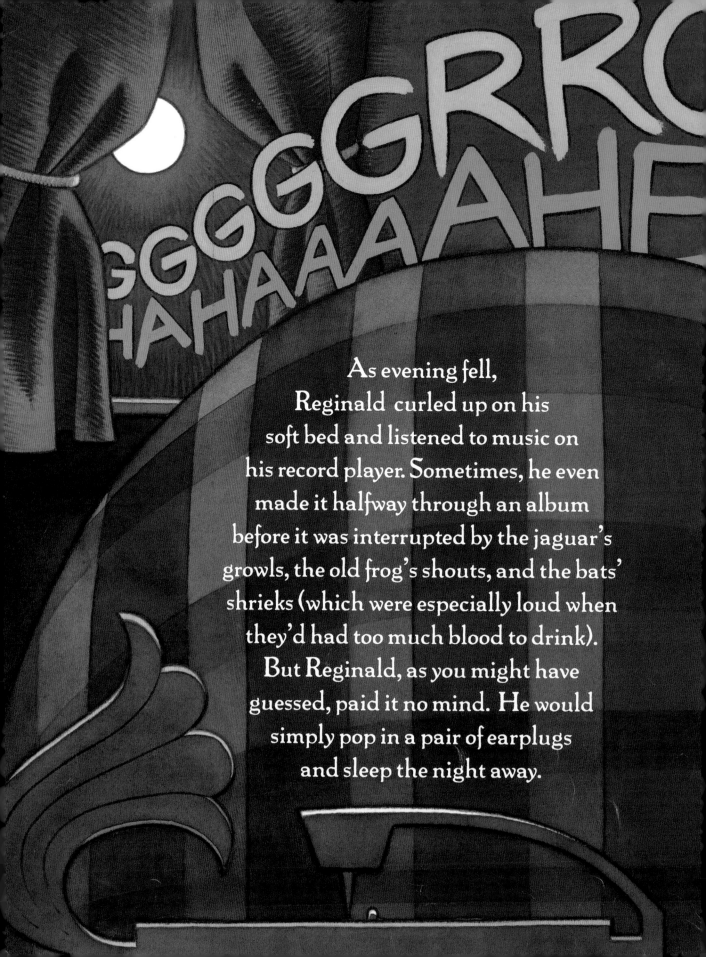

GGGGGRRRO
GGHAHAAAAHF

As evening fell,
Reginald curled up on his
soft bed and listened to music on
his record player. Sometimes, he even
made it halfway through an album
before it was interrupted by the jaguar's
growls, the old frog's shouts, and the bats'
shrieks (which were especially loud when
they'd had too much blood to drink).
But Reginald, as you might have
guessed, paid it no mind. He would
simply pop in a pair of earplugs
and sleep the night away.

On one particularly sizzling morning, Reginald decided to go for a swim, but when he reached the riverbank, he found every one of his neighbors— including the bats, who rarely came out during the day—lying about, trying to catch a cool breeze from the water.

When they saw Reginald, they burst out laughing, for he was dressed in the most ridiculous manner they had ever seen. The ape just smiled and waved a fork in the air. "I'm gonna eatcha," he said.

Reginald said nothing and slipped into the water,
where he proceeded to splash around for a bit.

"What do you think you're doing?" shouted the old frog.
It was the first time he had asked Reginald anything.

"The backstroke," replied Reginald,
and continued doing just that.

"Oh yeah, the backstroke," the old frog huffed. "We can do that too, right, boys?"

The geckos stared at each other. "Uh, no we can't, boss," said one of them.

"WHO SAID THAT?" the old frog screamed. "I'll show you! I can do the backstroke better than any cow!"

"Bull," said Reginald, correcting him.

The old frog's eyes bulged out of his head. "Are you calling me a liar? That's the last straw!" he shouted.

And with that, he hopped into the river on his back and started flipping about like a madman.

"You've got to loosen up, old frog," called Reginald. "Try kicking your legs out and twirling your arms slowly, like two windmills on a calm spring day."

Reluctantly, the old frog did as Reginald suggested, and before he knew it, he was doing the backstroke, too. "Weee-ha!" he cried. "This is great! You guys gotta come in and try it!"

The geckos were wary, but none dared disagree
with the old frog again. One by one, they filed into the
river, until they were all bobbing in front of Reginald.
"It's very simple," he said to them. "You must lie
flat on your back, kick your legs, and spin your arms
around like the hands of a clock." The geckos nodded
and spread out to practice.

"What's going on out there?" the bats screeched as they swooped down to the shore to see what the fuss was about. "What's all that noise?"

"We're doing the backstroke," replied Reginald. "Care to give it a try? I bet you'd like it."

Well, the bats could not resist a bet, so they tiptoed into the water, fully intending to tell Reginald that they hated the backstroke, no matter how it made them feel.

But by the time Reginald finished his instructions, the bats had forgotten all about their plan; they were too busy having fun to pretend that they weren't having fun.

All this frolicking infuriated the jaguar. He came to the edge of the water and fixed his eyes on Reginald.

"You can't trick me," he snarled. "I'll never swim with a COW!"

"Oh, cut the hooey," said the old frog, paddling up beside Reginald. "You'll never swim with anyone! You're afraid of getting wet!"

All at once, the jaguar deflated like a popped balloon. The other animals flew into a giggling fit.

"If any of you are interested in learning the
sidestroke someday, I suggest you stop that," said
Reginald. They became silent at once.

With a little encouragement, the jaguar slunk
into the river, straining to keep his head above water
as Reginald showed him the finer points of the
backstroke.

The animals swam together, and the afternoon came and went. Just before the sun began to sink in the sky, Reginald organized a race to see who could backstroke to the waterfall first.

The old frog was the winner, but Reginald complimented everyone on their efforts, especially the jaguar, who came in a respectable second. They all agreed to meet at the river on the next hot day, as long as Reginald would be there to teach them. He promised he would.

Then Reginald said his farewells and started off for home.

But when he reached the shore, he saw an enormous figure blocking his path into the jungle.

"I'm terribly sorry, ape. We seem to have forgotten you,"
said Reginald. "Would you like to learn the backstroke, too?"
The ape scratched his head.
"Mmmmm, nope," he decided. "I'd still rather eatcha."

Reginald shrugged. "You can't please everybody," he said. Then he went home to prepare an early evening snack.